Date Due

NOV - 6			
MAY 29			
NOV 3			

DATE	STUDENT NAME
NOV 27	

The Alden Family Mysteries
by Gertrude Chandler Warner

THE BOXCAR CHILDREN
SURPRISE ISLAND
THE YELLOW HOUSE MYSTERY
MYSTERY RANCH
MIKE'S MYSTERY
BLUE BAY MYSTERY
THE WOODSHED MYSTERY
THE LIGHTHOUSE MYSTERY
MOUNTAIN TOP MYSTERY
SCHOOLHOUSE MYSTERY
CABOOSE MYSTERY
HOUSEBOAT MYSTERY
SNOWBOUND MYSTERY
TREE HOUSE MYSTERY
BICYCLE MYSTERY
MYSTERY IN THE SAND
MYSTERY BEHIND THE WALL
BUS STATION MYSTERY
BENNY UNCOVERS A MYSTERY

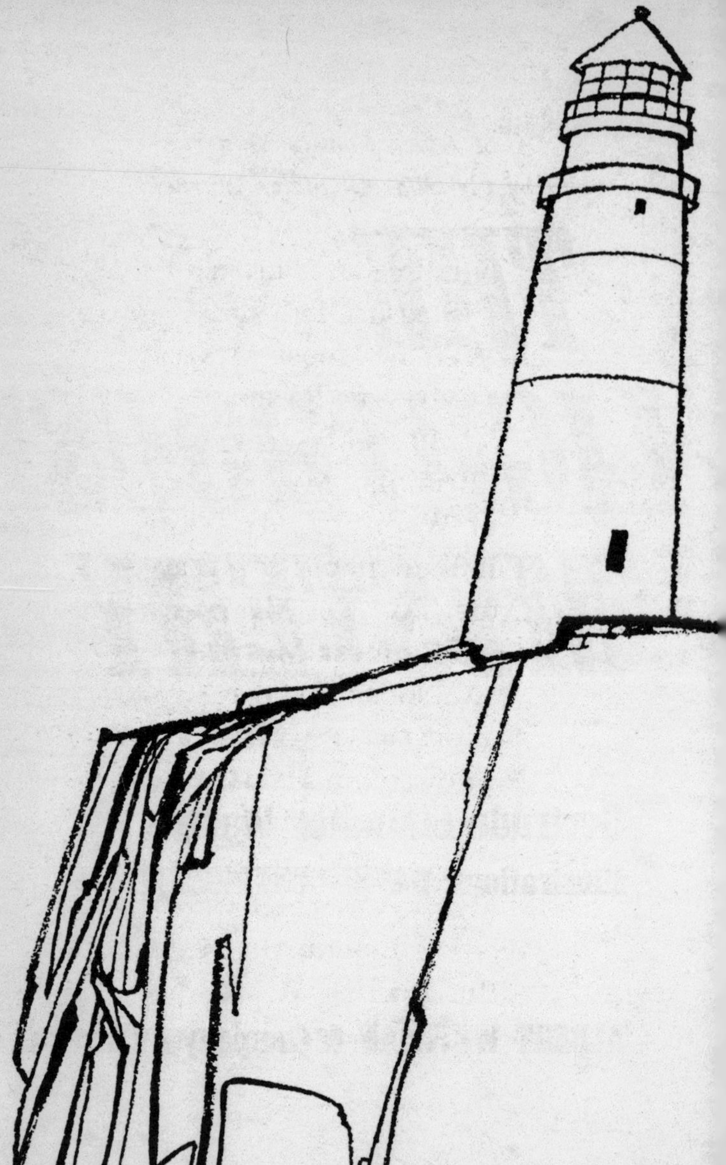

THE LIGHTHOUSE MYSTERY

Gertrude Chandler Warner
Illustrations: DAVID CUNNINGHAM

ALBERT WHITMAN & Company • Chicago

ISBN 0-8075-4546-5

1 3 5 7 9 10 8 6 4 2

Printed in the U.S.A.

Contents

CHAPTER 1

Lighthouse for Sale

The visit to Aunt Jane came to an end. Now, after so many years, Aunt Jane was married to Andy Bean. Nobody called her Mrs. Bean. This pleased her very much. Everyone called her Mrs. Andy, and that pleased Andy.

Grandfather Alden called his four grandchildren to him and said, "I think we should go home now. Aunt Jane and Andy want to go away on a wedding trip."

"I wonder where?" said Benny. "I bet they are going around the world. Andy told Aunt Jane that she would never have a dull moment."

Henry laughed. "I can believe that," he said. "Andy is never still."

Violet said, "Aunt Jane looks so young and well, doesn't she, Jessie?"

"Yes," agreed Jessie. "Ever since Uncle Andy came home she has been very happy. I agree with you, Grandfather. I think we ought to go. We don't want to stay on the farm without Aunt Jane."

So they packed their bags to go home. Aunt Jane helped Jessie make a picnic lunch.

All the good-bys were said and Henry started the car. "Here we go!" Benny cried.

And so they started for home—at least that was what they planned.

Henry said, "Let's have a change and go home by the beach road."

Henry drove the station wagon down the beach road. They could see the ocean most of the way. After about an hour Benny said, "I'm hungry."

"You are always hungry," said his grandfather. "Wait till we come to the lighthouse in Conley. There is a little store there. We could buy some milk. We have enough sandwiches to last two meals—ham and chicken. Aunt Jane makes delicious sandwiches."

"Let's go out and see the lighthouse," said Benny. "Maybe the lighthouse keeper would show us the little porch on the top floor."

"Maybe he would, old fellow," said Henry, laughing. "That is called a lookout, not a porch. But it is a long climb to the top of a lighthouse."

Soon they saw the lighthouse in the distance. It was white. There was a little white house near the foot of the lighthouse with a little path between. The two buildings stood on a rocky point of land, almost in the water.

"Look!" cried Violet. "There's a sign on it. What does it say?"

"I can't see yet," said Mr. Alden.

"I can," said Henry. "It says FOR SALE."

"A lighthouse for sale!" said Jessie. "I didn't know anyone ever sold lighthouses. I thought they belonged to the government."

"To the Coast Guard," said Mr. Alden. "But I have heard that many lighthouses are being sold. Radar is used to keep ships safe now."

"Oh, what a wonderful house that would be to live in, Grandfather!" said Benny. "See, there is a window on each floor. You could sleep on the first floor, and then you wouldn't have to do any climbing. The girls could have the next floor, and Henry the next, and I could have the top floor with that little porch—I mean lookout. That would be neat!"

Mr. Alden laughed. He said, "Are you saying you want to buy the lighthouse?"

"Oh, absolutely!" said Benny.

"Really," said Jessie, "we could have a lovely time in a lighthouse, Grandfather. We could go swimming any time right in our own yard."

"And we could pick up shells and study the water birds," said Violet quietly.

"We could certainly go fishing," added Henry.

They had come to the lighthouse by this time. Henry stopped the car, and they all looked at the place. Nobody said a word. They were all waiting for Grandfather to make up his mind.

At last he said, "Come on, children, we'll go into

the little store and ask some questions. Maybe we *could* use a lighthouse."

"Hurray!" shouted Benny.

Everyone else was as pleased as Benny. They smiled and looked at each other.

"Drive right up to the door," said Mr. Alden. "A store man always knows everything."

It was true. When Mr. Alden said, "What do you know about that lighthouse?" the man laughed and said, "I know everything about that lighthouse. It's not used any more."

"I see it's for sale," said Mr. Alden.

"Well, it isn't for sale now," said the man, "because I bought it myself. I haven't had time to take down the sign. I'd like to rent it, though."

"Would you?" asked Mr. Alden. "My grandchildren think they would like to spend a few weeks there."

"Well, I'd be glad to rent it to you. It's all fixed up for light housekeeping."

Benny laughed. "Light housekeeping in a lighthouse," he said. "That's a good joke."

"Does the little white house go with it?" asked Henry.

"Well, no," said the storekeeper. "It ought to. But I wasn't quick enough to buy the house. A man named Cook bought that. He buys houses and sells them. He is going to fix it up to rent someday. But now the windows are broken, as maybe you saw, and they are all boarded up. He never thought anyone would rent the lighthouse."

"Won't we need the little house?" asked Jessie.

"No. That was the summer kitchen. The winter kitchen in the lighthouse is all right. It really has a better gas stove and refrigerator. There's a good cot bed on every floor. You could get all your food right here in my store. My name is Hall."

"I thought so, Mr. Hall, when I saw the sign HALL'S GROCERY," said Mr. Alden.

Henry asked, "Could we ever build a fire on the beach for a cook-out?"

"Yes, you could. There's nothing on that point

but sand and water and rocks. No bushes. You will be careful, I know."

Benny said, "Yes, we bury our fires with sand."

"Good! Make yourselves at home. Do anything you want. Here's the key if you want to go in and look around."

"Well, I do," said Benny. "I want to see the top floor with the porch railing."

"Fine," said Grandfather. "You get in the car. I'll settle the rent with Mr. Hall."

Henry took the key and drove down to the lighthouse. They could not drive to the door because the road was too sandy.

When Henry unlocked the door, the girls went into the kitchen at once.

"Good!" said Jessie, "this is a fine little gas stove."

Violet said, "The dishes are all different, but we like them different."

Benny climbed the winding stairs. Round and round he went.

He called, "These rooms are very small. Nothing but a cot bed in each one." He stopped to look out of each window. He called out, "First floor. This is Grandfather's room."

He climbed higher. "Second floor, Jessie and Violet. Third floor, Henry. And here's mine!" They could hardly hear him.

Then they heard no more at all from Benny. He was out on his top floor looking out to sea.

Grandfather said, "It's lucky there's a window on every floor. It will be hot in here."

"Maybe not too hot," said Violet. "We are right by the sea breezes."

By the time the beds were made, everyone was tired.

"Let's go to bed," said Mr. Alden.

"Go to bed at eight o'clock?" cried Benny. "But I guess my bed will feel rather nice after all."

Everyone was soon asleep. No one heard the town clock strike. But it did strike—nine, ten, eleven. As it struck twelve, Watch sat up and began to bark.

CHAPTER 2

Unfriendly Characters

Watch always slept at the foot of Jessie's bed.

"Keep still, Watch!" said Jessie. "You'll wake everybody up!"

But Watch didn't stop. He barked all the more. His hair stood up straight around his neck.

Benny came down the stairs. Henry came. Mr. Alden called, "What's the matter with Watch, Jessie?"

"I don't know, Grandfather," called Jessie. "He must hear something he doesn't like."

Benny began to pat the dog. "What's the matter with you, Watch? Why do you have to bark at twelve o'clock midnight? Why couldn't you bark at four o'clock in the afternoon? Then we could do something about it."

Watch barked on and on. He stopped just long enough to growl.

Suddenly Benny said, "I smell steak and mashed potatoes."

"Benny, mashed potatoes don't smell," said Violet.

"I can smell them," said Benny.

"Are you sure it is not baked potatoes you smell?" asked Henry. "I don't smell anything."

"No. Baked potatoes smell even better. Maybe it's the milk and butter and pepper and salt that I smell."

"Well, maybe pepper, Benny. Certainly not salt," said Jessie.

Henry was frowning. "Maybe someone is hiding and eating in that little house at the foot of our lighthouse. But I thought it was empty," he said.

Just then Watch stopped barking. He lay down and put his head on his paws and shut his eyes. Everyone was surprised.

"Just look at Watch now," said Jessie. "He

doesn't care any more. I guess the danger is over, whatever it was."

"That's a funny thing," said Benny. He started upstairs.

"It's more than funny, Ben," said Henry. "The dog must have heard something."

"We'll find out tomorrow," said Mr. Alden. "I'll ask the police."

Then everyone went back to bed. Violet thought she could not go back to sleep, but she did.

They slept till morning. After a rather poor breakfast, Jessie said, "Well, the first thing is to go to the store and buy food."

"Right," said her grandfather. He missed his morning coffee and toast.

No one spoke of the midnight noise. With the sun shining, it seemed as if nothing had happened.

As they walked up the street to the grocery store they saw a middle-aged man coming. He had sharp, black eyes. He did not even look at the Aldens. He passed Jessie, almost bumping her.

"Well!" said Benny, when the man had gone by. "He's a queer character."

"He did look at us sideways," said Violet. "I saw him when he was far down the street."

"But why should he almost bump into Jessie?" Henry asked. "He might have knocked her down if she hadn't moved quickly. A queer character is right, Ben."

"I think we notice everybody now," said Violet. "We think they are a part of our mystery."

Suddenly everyone was thinking about the noise in the night. It had been real!

"Right!" said Henry. He took Violet's arm as they went into the store. "You are always right."

There was only one person in the store. It was a boy of about Henry's age. Under his arm he had a college book. Henry knew it at once.

The girls started to buy groceries, but Henry gave the boy a friendly smile and said, "I noticed your book. Do you go to college?"

"I certainly don't," said the boy loudly. Then he

went out of the store and banged the door.

"Hey, what's the matter with *him?"* asked Henry. He stared after the boy.

"He's looking for trouble, that feller!" said Benny. His voice sounded just like his grandfather's.

Mr. Hall said, "He doesn't have to look for trouble. He's got trouble."

"What trouble?" asked Henry. "He looks so cross at everybody."

"Well, his father won't let him go to school," said Mr. Hall.

"School?" cried Benny. "He *wants* to go to school, and his father won't *let* him?"

"That's right," said Mr. Hall.

Benny said, "Didn't that boy go to high school?"

"Oh, yes, he had to go to high school. It's the law. He's very smart, especially in science. He got through high school at sixteen."

"Well," said Henry, "he is smart, then. But he's looking for trouble. It wouldn't hurt him to be

polite to a stranger."

"He isn't polite to anybody," said Mr. Hall. "I try to be nice to him, but you see how he acts. He doesn't want friends."

"Now *that* is too bad," said Benny. "Everyone ought to have friends."

"I guess it isn't hard for you to make friends," said Mr. Hall. He laughed.

"No, it isn't," said Benny. "I'm lucky. We're all lucky."

Henry was quiet. At last he said, "I wish we could do something with that father. A boy like that ought to go to college if he wants to."

"He wants to all right. That's all he thinks about —college—college—and I guess whatever lives in the sea. He's always picking up shells or bits of seaweed. Now I say if any boy wants to learn, let him learn."

"Right," said Benny. "There are lots of boys I know that don't want to learn."

"I don't think you can do anything with his

father," Mr. Hall said. "You're not the first people who have tried."

Then the four Aldens thought of the same name —Grandfather. But they did not say it. Grandfather knew how to get things done.

"That boy is another queer character," said Benny. "Two cross people in ten minutes." Benny did not see many cross people.

Then Mr. Alden said, "By the way, Mr. Hall, our dog barked in the night. We feel that someone was prowling about. I thought I'd see the police today."

Mr. Hall shook his head. "No police in this town," he said. "Never had any trouble here."

"No police!" said Mr. Alden. "I never heard of such a thing. Who looks up a mystery?"

"Nobody, I guess. Never had a mystery either."

As the Aldens drove home, they were all thinking.

Grandfather said, "I suppose I could send for John Carter."

"Oh, please don't," cried Benny. "We want to find out for ourselves. No police, no Mr. Carter, no help at all!"

"Very well," said Grandfather with a smile.

"We'll have to solve the mystery, Ben," said Henry.

"Maybe we can do it better than Mr. Carter can," said Benny.

"Oh," said Jessie. "Somebody thinks he's pretty smart, Mr. Benny! But we all know that Mr. Carter is right there. He would come to help us in a minute."

When they reached the lighthouse with the groceries, Jessie said, "I wonder just the same about that black-eyed man and the cross boy. Could one of them have anything to do with our mystery?"

"I don't see how," said Benny. "But you never know. Maybe they are cooking up something or other."

Benny didn't know then how near he was to the truth.

CHAPTER 3

Cement for a Project

Jessie boiled a dozen eggs and a dozen potatoes. She put them in the refrigerator. By noon she had made an enormous potato salad. She had bought rolls and butter and a cherry pie.

"Let's eat lunch out on the rocks," she said. "It's too hot in the lighthouse. You carry the salad, Henry. And, Benny, you carry the cherry pie and the knife."

They found a fine seat for Grandfather that just fitted him. "Really, this is an easy chair," he said, "made out of rocks."

The other seats were not so easy. The rocks were sharp. The table was not very flat either.

"I have an idea," shouted Benny suddenly. "Let's find stones and make five easy chairs. Then build up the table with a flat stone. And then get some cement and fill in the cracks."

"A wonderful idea, Ben," said Henry. "A small bag of cement would be enough. We've got plenty of sand."

"I saw a place where they had cement," said Violet. "Some men were building a driveway."

"Where?" asked Benny.

"Well, don't you remember when we came from Aunt Jane's there was a big new gas station where some men were building a driveway?"

"I remember it," said Mr. Alden. "It was right beside a little fish market."

"Let's go the minute lunch is over," said Benny.

"Lunch is over for me right now," said Mr. Alden. He ate the last of his cherry pie. "The ocean will wash away the crumbs."

Jessie and Henry picked up all the dishes and washed them in the sea. Then Henry backed the car out and they all went down to the little fish market. Sure enough, the men were at work on the driveway. Bags of cement were lying around.

"Where can we buy some cement?" asked

Henry, stopping the car. He put his head out of the window.

"How much do you want?" asked the man who was the foreman.

"Well, we want to make some seats and a table down on the rocks by the lighthouse. How much would you think we'd need?"

"Take this small bag," said the foreman. "Bring back what you don't want."

Henry said, "Is it three parts of sand to one part of cement?"

"Right," said the foreman. "You can borrow this hoe if you want."

"That's neat!" cried Benny. "I'll hoe!"

"Wish I could come and help you," said the man, smiling. He looked at the laughing family. They all laughed again. Henry lifted the bag into the car, and Benny took the hoe.

"I'll put the cement on Violet's feet," said Henry. But he was joking.

Then the Aldens noticed that one of the men

was staring at them with big, black eyes. It was the same man who had almost bumped into Jessie.

When he saw that they knew him, the man turned his back and began to work again.

After they had driven away, Jessie could not help saying, "That was odd seeing that man again." Everyone agreed.

"Stop at the store, Henry, and buy a trowel," said Grandfather. "You'll have to smooth the cement and carry it to the rocks."

When the Aldens got back to the lighthouse they went to the rocks at once. The only seat which was comfortable already was Mr. Alden's. They

walked around trying to find big rocks of the right shape. Benny sat down on every seat he could find to try it. Then the boys began to carry big stones and the girls took the little stones to fill the cracks. At last they had five seats around a fine table.

Henry began to mix the cement. "Not with salt water," he said. "We must have fresh water."

He found a big rock that was shaped like a tub. He mixed the cement in that.

"Now let me hoe it, Henry," begged Benny. "I know just how to do it. I watched the men."

"Don't mix up too much at first," said Jessie. "It will get hard before we finish all the seats."

"Isn't this fun?" cried Benny, hoeing away. "Just like making mud pies. Let's do Violet's seat first. She has such a comfortable looking chair already." So they carried the cement in a newspaper and Benny plastered the seat and smoothed it with the trowel.

"Isn't that wonderful!" said Violet. "I'd love to try it."

"Better not," said Henry. "Let it dry overnight."

Then Jessie and Henry took turns with the trowel, and at last they all helped Benny with his own seat and the table.

"Let's make places for cups on the table," said Violet. So when the cement on the table was soft and smooth she pressed a cup into it in five places. The mark made a wonderful saucer. The cup could not fall off.

"Plates, too!" said Benny.

With a stick he drew B for Benny, J for Jessie, V for Violet, H for Henry, and G for grandfather beside the plates.

The cement was almost gone, but they took the bag back to the workmen and Henry paid the foreman for it. He gave back the hoe. They noticed that the black-eyed man was not there.

"I'm glad," said Benny as they drove back, "I don't like him anyway."

"I wonder who he is," said Mr. Alden.

It was not too long before he found out.

CHAPTER 4

A Midnight Visitor

It was delightful to sit on the beach that evening even though they could not use their new seats. The family sat there long after supper watching the sunset.

Gulls flew overhead and landed on the rocks near by.

Suddenly Henry said, "It's queer how sleepy we get."

"It's the sea air," said Mr. Alden. "Go to bed anytime you want."

In fact, the whole family went to bed at nine o'clock and were asleep very soon after.

The Conley town clock struck as it always did. Ten, eleven, twelve. And then Watch began to whine. His hair stood up along his back and around his neck. He began to howl.

"No, Watch," said Benny. "If you're going to howl every night at midnight, you might as well go home. You're no help to us."

But Watch went right on howling.

"I wonder if someone is cooking in that little house," said Henry.

"No one's there," said Benny. "We would have heard him go crunch, crunch, crunch on those little stones."

"That house is all boarded up anyway," said Jessie. "The door must be locked and the windows don't open. Nobody could be in there."

"Someone might take off a board and get in a window," said Henry. "Then he could put the board back every night. Tomorrow we'll take a look." Benny wanted to go right down. But just then Watch began to quiet down. He gave a last growl and went to sleep.

"You're a funny dog," said Benny. "See that you keep still the rest of the night."

But it was not Watch who kept Jessie and Violet

awake a little longer. When Jessie turned out her light she looked out of her window. In the moonlight she saw a woman walking quietly away. Her feet did not go crunch, crunch. She walked softly in the tall beach grass.

Jessie called quietly to Violet. She came and looked out, too.

"A woman!" she whispered. "What do you suppose she is doing here?"

"She's going away at least," answered Jessie. "We certainly don't need to get Benny down again. And Watch is quiet. Look, Violet. She is hiding behind those bushes before she goes up the street."

The street was empty. The stores were dark. Very soon the woman went quietly up the road and out of sight. The two girls went back to bed and fell asleep.

About dawn Watch growled softly. But everyone was sleeping deeply. No one awoke.

In the morning Jessie called everyone to breakfast out on the rocks.

"I know my place," said Benny, "on account of the B."

When everything was eaten, the girls told their strange story about the woman.

Mr. Alden said, "I think we had better look that

little house over. Everyone can help. Try each board to see if it is loose."

The Aldens began with the front windows and found everything tight. The door was locked. There was no loose window board. Watch trotted along quietly and did not bark.

"It's funny," said Jessie, "that Watch doesn't bark."

"Maybe there's nothing for him to bark at now," said Mr. Alden. "Certainly this house is shut tight."

"Hey! Look at this!" said Henry suddenly. He caught a sheet of paper that was blowing down to the sand. The paper was marked into little squares. There were numbers and strange letters in each. Sometimes there were question marks.

"That doesn't mean a thing to me," said Jessie.

"Me either," agreed Henry. "But I think somebody is pretty clever. It looks like college science work, but I don't understand it. It's not in my studies so far."

"Just as if someone were testing something," said Violet slowly. "Like an experiment."

"Exactly!" cried Henry. He smiled at his little sister. "But how does it fit in with cooking smells and your seeing a woman at night?"

"Keep that paper, Henry," said Mr. Alden as they went back to the rocks.

Just then Violet spoke of the shells.

"The beach is covered with them," cried Benny

He jumped off the rocks to the sand. "I know this one. It's a clam shell, and this one is a scallop shell."

"Here's a queer one," said Jessie. "It has five toes."

"That's a cat's paw," said Mr. Alden. "See how many kinds we can find."

Mr. Alden knew all about shells, as well as about birds and flowers.

They found a snail shell, a slipper shell, and gold and silver colored shells. In all they found fourteen different kinds.

"There's plenty of seaweed here, too," Benny said. "But who would want to collect that? Maybe that cross boy would find it interesting."

"This makes me think of Blue Bay," said Violet, smiling. "We ate out of shells there."

"But this is safer for swimming than Blue Bay," said Henry. "No sharks here."

Jessie said slowly, "It's too bad we don't have swim suits. I suppose four new suits would cost too much."

"No," said her grandfather, "you need new ones anyway. And you mustn't be on the beach and not go swimming."

"Maybe Mr. Hall has some suits," Jessie went on. "He has almost everything."

She smiled to think of suits and groceries and everything else mixed together in the little store.

They put their shells on the rock table and walked over to the store.

"No," said Mr. Hall, "I haven't any swim suits. But there is a lady down the street who sells hats.

She has suits, too. You'll see the sign as you go out."

Benny said, "I saw the sign when I came in. It said 'HATS'—and that's where we go to buy bathing suits? That's funny."

"Well," said Mr. Hall with a laugh, "my sign says 'GROCERIES' and people come here to buy paint and wallpaper."

They went out of the store and down the street. The dock was near by and Benny pulled Henry over to see the boats. "Look at that one," he said. "She's a beauty. Her name's Sea Cook II."

Henry said, "I guess a boat like that isn't too big for one man to run. You're right, Benny, she is a beauty."

Just then Jessie and Violet called to the boys. The girls were more interested in suits than boats. The boys saw Grandfather waiting with the girls. Together the Aldens looked in the window of the hat shop. There were beautiful summer hats in the window—and one suit. It was blue.

"There's your suit, Jessie, if it fits," said Henry. "Of course, Ben wants red."

"Right," said Benny. "Red is my color."

The lady in the hat shop smiled to see the whole family coming in. She said her name was Mrs. Ross.

Suddenly Henry looked out of the window. The black-eyed man was going by.

"Do you know who that man is?" Henry asked.

"Oh, yes, indeed. His name is Tom Cook."

"What does he do for a living?" asked Mr. Alden.

"He's really a fisherman. But sometimes the fishing is poor, so he works on odd jobs. They say he has made a fortune selling lobsters and renting houses to the summer people."

"He doesn't look it, does he?" said Henry. "He looks poor."

"He saves his money," said Mrs. Ross. "He won't spend a cent. He has a fine boat and he won't let his son use it, and his son is no little boy. He's seventeen years old already."

An idea hit Benny, but he didn't say anything aloud. The man was a Mr. Cook. That beautiful boat was the Sea Cook II. It must be the black-eyed man's boat.

Henry was thinking, too. That first day they had met Mr. Hall and rented the lighthouse—hadn't he said a man named Cook had bought the summer kitchen? Maybe here was another clue.

"Too bad," said Jessie.

"Yes, it's too bad. The boy does use it, though. People say that he is always taking that boat out after dark. They say he has some fancy idea in his head. Nobody knows what it is. He always comes back carrying something. Sometimes it is a small thing like a jar, and sometimes a great big thing like a barrel. At least that's what I'm told."

"I wonder what it is?" said Benny.

"I haven't the least idea," said Mrs. Ross. "He goes way out. Out of sight. His father doesn't know he takes the boat, though how the boy has kept him from finding out, I don't know."

"I bet some day he's going to find out," said Benny. "Then there will be trouble."

"Trouble?" cried Mrs. Ross. "There's enough trouble already in that house between Mr. Cook and his son. The mother stands up for the boy. The father will hardly speak to his own son."

"Why?" asked Mr. Alden.

"Well, you see this boy is very smart. He finished high school at sixteen. He's been just hanging around ever since. His father won't let him work. Too proud. And the boy wants to go away to college. His father won't let him."

"Oh, my!" said Benny. "That's the cross boy we saw in the store, and the cross man with the black eyes is his father. That explains a lot, doesn't it, Grandfather?"

"Yes, Benny. Those two will always be in trouble unless we do something about it."

"Did you say 'we'?" asked Henry in surprise.

"Yes, *we*," answered Mr. Alden with a smile.

CHAPTER 5

Little House with a Secret

The Aldens went right back to their lighthouse with the new suits. They put them on at once and went out to their own little white beach.

"Be careful now," said Mr. Alden. "You don't know this beach, and you must find out how deep the water is."

"Mr. Hall says it is very deep on the other side of the lighthouse," said Henry. "But it is not over your head on this side. I asked him."

"I like it deep," said Benny, swimming away.

Every one of the Aldens could swim very well. Henry and Jessie could dive. But this was no place to dive. It was too rocky.

The water was cool, but the day was hot. Mr. Alden sat in his own rock chair and watched the swimmers. They threw water and swam under water. Even Watch swam around, barking for fun.

"You bark all you want to now, Watch," said Violet, laughing. "Just keep still at midnight tonight." She really had no idea that Watch would bark every single night.

That night the family sat up late. It was dark when Benny went climbing up to his top floor. He put on light blue pajamas and went out on his little lookout. He sat down in a beach chair.

Benny did not know that he showed up plainly in the moonlight in his light pajamas.

He was looking at the stars. They looked very bright here because there were no street lights. Then one star moved. Soon Benny knew that it was not a star but a light on a boat. The boat was coming in. Suddenly the boat stopped and turned around and went out to sea again.

"Well, well," thought Benny. "Whoever he is, he changed his mind."

Ideas began to spin around in Benny's head. He

remembered what Mrs. Ross in the hat shop had said. He thought about seeing the Sea Cook at the dock.

Then next he thought, "I wonder if he saw me from his boat. I bet he did. I bet it's our Cook boy with his father's boat. That boat is certainly a beauty."

Benny jumped up to turn out his light. He put on a dark coat and watched at the window. Very soon the boat turned around again and came in to the dock not far from the lighthouse. It looked like a man who jumped out. But Benny knew that the Cook boy was as big as a man. Benny watched him as he bent over his boat. He took out a pail.

"A pail this time," thought Benny. "I do wonder what is in it."

But he didn't find out. The boy looked all around. The whole town had gone to bed. The boy took the pail and disappeared up the street. Benny went to bed. If he had watched a little longer he would have seen more. But he was soon asleep.

At midnight Watch began to bark.

"Oh, my, Watch!" cried Jessie. "I guess you are going to bark every night. But you'll stop in about ten minutes. So bark away."

That is just what the dog did. He barked and howled for ten minutes and then he went back to sleep.

Violet said, "You're just like a baby, Watch! You wake us up every night crying."

Several hours later Watch growled softly but nobody heard.

For the next few days no one was surprised to hear Watch bark during the night. No one got up. They knew Watch would bark for about ten minutes and then he would stop.

But one morning Henry said, "I don't like it, just the same." He frowned. "The dog must hear something."

The girls said they had seen the woman again going away very quietly. She had a bag in her hand.

Henry said, "I am going to find out why that woman comes here. I'm going to hunt all over this point of land."

"We'll help you," said Jessie.

On the other side of the lighthouse, behind the little summer kitchen, there were enormous rocks. The land went downhill to the water. The young Aldens hunted over every inch of land to find some way to get into the house. They found nothing.

Then Henry said, "Let's look at those boards nailed over the windows. There must be a crack somewhere. Maybe we can see in."

They all looked up at the windows. "Do you see that board high up?" asked Jessie, pointing. "There's a big crack there, but it's too high to see through."

"Good for you, Jess," said Henry. "I see what you mean. I am not tall enough, but Benny will be."

"What do you mean?" asked Violet, laughing a little. "You are much taller than Benny."

"Well, Ben," said Henry, laughing, too, "I'll

bend over and you stand on my back and look through the crack."

"Oh, boy!" said Benny. He climbed up on Henry's back like a monkey and stood up. He put

his hands around his eyes and peeked in the crack.

"I can see quite well," Benny said, "because there is another big crack in the front door we didn't find. Oh, somebody does cook here!" he shouted. "There is a stove and a frying pan on it. There are pails of water on the floor with something brown in the water. There's a little microscope on the table. It's no good. It's too small. I bet it cost about three dollars. Then there are a lot of papers with little squares like the one we found. Books and other stuff, too."

"Good!" said Jessie in excitement. "See if you can tell what is in the pails."

"It's seaweed," cried Benny. "It's all over the floor, and some is hanging over the edge of the kettle near the stove."

"What a queer thing," said Violet. "I wonder what it all means."

"Certainly it means that somebody comes here at night and makes the dog bark," said Henry.

"That woman?" asked Jessie.

"You sound funny, Henry, upside down," said Benny. "There are plates and cups on the shelf and it looks like a bag of flour."

"Better get down now, Ben," said Henry. "You are getting heavy."

Benny jumped down lightly.

"There was one pail under the window I couldn't see very well," said Benny. "But it looked as if there's something glowing in it."

"Glowing?" asked Henry. "What can that be? Wait a minute. Do you remember how we saw something glowing in the water near Blue Bay? It was plankton, I think."

"I bet it is," said Benny. "We saw that under the microscope going to Blue Bay. All tiny fishes and eggs and things you can't see."

"That's what the microscope here is for," said Henry slowly. "To study the plankton and seaweed."

"We don't know much more than we did," said Jessie. "We just know someone—a woman—

comes to work here every night. I suppose it could be some kind of hobby."

"But the woman comes at midnight and goes away in ten minutes," put in Benny. "How does that fit in? Nobody can do much in ten minutes."

Henry said, "It seems to me there is no danger from someone who studies seaweed. Maybe the person's afraid of something."

"Isn't it strange, Henry?" asked Violet. "You said there's a stove there, and we've smelled something cooking at night."

"Well, I don't know," said Henry, thinking. "I have heard that seaweed could be food for cows and horses and pigs. But they won't eat it. It tastes awful."

"Wait!" said Benny. "I saw something else. I saw some bags on the shelf. They looked like bags of flour and sugar. There were others with no labels."

"Now what do you think those are for?" asked Violet.

"Maybe someone is trying to make seaweed taste

good," said Jessie, half joking about the thought. "Well, let's go. Grandfather may have some ideas."

Mr. Alden heard the strange story. And he did have a small idea. "I was talking to Mr. Hall about the Cook boy, and he says he often sleeps all the morning."

"Well," said Jessie, "you remember Mrs. Ross told us the Cook boy takes his father's boat out at night. That's why he sleeps days."

Suddenly Benny said, "Am I dumb! I had a clue and I didn't fit it with the others. I was thinking about a woman in the summer kitchen because that's all we have seen."

He stopped, but Henry said, "Go on."

Benny asked, "You remember when I thought I saw the Cook boy get out of his father's boat and carry a pail away? I thought he went off up the street. I bet if I had watched I would have seen him come back into the summer kitchen. That Cook boy *and* the woman have something to do with our mystery."

Henry said, "That paper with the squares that looked like a college experiment could belong to the Cook boy. If he is coming around here at night, that explains how we found it here."

"Maybe we ought to put that paper back through the window, Henry," said Benny. "The Cook boy may need it."

"No, Ben," said Henry. "If we put it back, he will know that someone has been there. And it isn't time yet to tell him that. We have to make friends with him first. Then we can tell him we'd like to know more about what he is doing."

"And how in the world are we going to make friends with that cross boy? I should like to know," said Benny. "He doesn't want friends. He said so."

"Maybe he did say so," agreed Henry. "But I think he does want friends, even if he doesn't know it himself."

CHAPTER 6

Well Done for Benny

"Let's have a picnic," said Violet after the Aldens had made as many guesses as they could about what went on in the summer kitchen.

"We have a picnic every meal, I should say," said Benny. "We always eat outdoors on our own rocks."

"Well, I mean a real picnic," said Violet, "with a fire and hamburgers."

"Good for you, Violet," said Henry, smiling. "I'm all for it. You mean a real cook-out."

"I don't want hamburgers this time. I want frankfurters," said Benny.

"You can have two if you want. Or three," said Jessie. "And this time let's get a real fire going and not be in a hurry. It cooks better when it has burned down."

They went to the store and bought long rolls, big sweet pickles, and brownies as well as the meat. They left Watch outside.

Suddenly they heard him bark.

"Oh, boy," said Benny. "He's barking just the way he does in the night."

They all rushed out and Jessie called, "Stop it, Watch! Come here!"

Then they saw that he was barking at the Cook boy.

"He won't bite," said Jessie. She smiled at the boy. "He just barks."

Watch came to Jessie when she called, but he still growled in his throat. Violet could see that the boy did not like this.

"You don't need to be afraid of Watch," she said. "He's a very gentle dog. He would never bite anybody."

"I bet he would, though," said the boy, "if anyone tried to hurt you kids."

He went quickly down the street and Watch still

growled. No one had time to say anything more to the boy.

"Now that is very funny," said Benny. "Watch did bark just exactly as he does at night. I bet that Cook boy *is* the one who is cooking seaweed."

Jessie laughed. "You said once that somebody was cooking up something. And it turned out to be true. It's the *Cook boy!*"

"Now I'm sure of it," said Henry quietly. "There aren't very many people in Conley who would be smart enough or interested enough to make those figures on that squared paper. The question is, what is he trying to do? And how does a woman fit into the puzzle?"

"Well, we can't do anything about it now," said Benny. "Let's go on with our picnic."

"Is this picnic going to be lunch or supper, Violet?"

"Oh, lunch! We couldn't wait for supper, now we are all set."

The Aldens went down on the beach and picked

up dry sticks of all sizes. Henry and Benny made a fireplace of stones. They put the sticks in the hole with papers and dry seaweed.

"No danger of fire here on the sand," said Henry. "We have the whole ocean to put it out."

At last the fire burned down to hot coals. It was hard to wait, but they did.

Jessie gave Benny a long straight fork to cook his frankfurter on. He stuck the frankfurter on the end and put it over the fire. He had no sooner done this than the frankfurter slipped off.

"Look at your frankfurter, Ben!" cried Henry. "It's in the fire!"

"Oh, so it is," cried Benny. He stuck his fork in again and lifted it out. The frankfurter was burning on one side.

"I like it burned," he said. He blew out the fire.

"But not burned up," said Mr. Alden, laughing. As he spoke, plop! went the frankfurter again.

"Do you want me to help you, Benny?" asked Jessie laughing, too.

"No, indeed! Thank you! If I can't cook a frankfurter, I'm a monkey."

"Well, I guess you're a monkey then," teased Henry, "for there goes your frankfurter."

Benny picked it up again. "You stay on!" he said to the frankfurter.

"Watch out, Ben! Ooops! There she goes!" cried Henry. He couldn't help laughing. The poor frankfurter was black all over.

This time just as Benny was putting it on the fork it slipped off again—swoosh!

"This time I'll hold my fork the other way," said Benny. His face was red with the hot fire. "I guess I can eat my own cooking."

He put the frankfurter into a roll and began to eat it. "Delicious!" he said, chewing happily.

"Please don't eat it, Ben," Henry begged. "You can have another and maybe it won't slip off. You can put it on our grill this time."

"No," said Benny. "No grill for me. I have to put it on a long fork. That's the way to cook a frankfurter."

"What does it taste like, Ben?" asked Henry, laughing.

"Coal," said Benny. "Delicious coal."

"Maybe charcoal," said Violet. "That's what it really is. I hope you'll try another one and have a decent lunch."

Benny was standing up on a rock eating brownies. He looked toward the street. There was the Cook boy going past.

"Hi!" shouted Benny. "Hello!"

The boy did answer. It was a very gruff hello. Then he went along.

Henry said thoughtfully, "It might be that he's more afraid than cross—afraid someone will stop his secret work."

Benny jumped down. "You know I think that Cook boy would like to come and eat with us. But he would never do it. I saw his face before he saw me. He looked as if he wished he could eat at our picnic."

"Very likely you are right," said Mr. Alden. "Maybe you can get to be friends little by little."

But as it turned out, something happened suddenly—not little by little.

CHAPTER 7

Baked Beans and Chowder

Henry went to the store to get the paper. He nearly bumped into the Cook boy coming out. The angry look on his face kept Henry from even trying to say hello.

"What's up now?" Henry wondered. Then he forgot about the boy because a sign on the store door said:

VILLAGE SUPPER. JULY 25TH.

Henry said to Mr. Hall, "What's this supper on the twenty-fifth?"

Mr. Hall sat down and said, "Oh, every July this village has a chowder supper outdoors. Everybody in town comes. We have chowder and baked beans, hot rolls and coffee, pies and cakes. It costs one dollar."

"It sounds good," said Henry. "Can anybody come?"

"Oh, yes. We want all the money we can get. We are trying to put in street lights. This year I think we will do it. All the tickets will be sold in one day. Everybody wants to come."

"I had better buy five tickets now," said Henry. "My family will all love to come."

"Here you are," said Mr. Hall. He gave Henry five tickets. "I'll tell you something else, too. You'll be surprised. Guess who makes the chowder and coffee and baked beans? Larry Cook! You see he isn't all bad. He does this every year. He loves to cook."

"Imagine that," said Henry. "I wouldn't think it."

"No, that Larry Cook is a surprise in many ways."

"Well, so he is," said Henry, thinking. "I met him as I came into the store. He seemed crosser than ever."

"Want to know why?" asked Mr. Hall. "Every year two summer people come up and help him.

This year they sent word they can't come. That's why Larry is crosser than ever. He can't do this alone with such a big crowd. Everybody else is busy making pies."

"I wonder if we could help him?" said Henry. "We would do just as he said. Maybe that would cheer him up."

"I'm sure it would. Your family would be a big help."

Henry went home with the tickets and the paper and the news. Everyone wanted to help Larry.

"I think Mr. Hall will tell him what I said," said Henry. "But if we meet him, we'll tell him, too."

"I heard something new about Larry's father," said Benny. "He is night watchman sometimes at the shipyard. So off and on he is busy all night. Maybe that's why he doesn't know his boat is gone."

Later that day the Aldens walked over to the dock. They met Larry. He went by them with a gruff hello.

Benny said, "Wait a minute, Larry. Would you like some help with your supper? We can peel onions and potatoes, and we all know how to get clams out of the shells."

"Do you?" asked Larry. He almost smiled. "There will sure be a lot of clams. I can't do it alone."

"Then we can help?" asked Benny.

"Yes, I'd be glad of your help," said Larry.

"Grandfather will help, too," said Jessie. "He is fine at getting out clams."

"Well, well!" said Larry. "I never thought Mr. Alden would be working for me, that's sure. You come around at nine Saturday morning, and we'll all get to work."

When Saturday came, the five Aldens went to meet Larry behind the store. There was a big field there, with a place for cooking and a tent for shelter. Other men had set up the long tables and chairs.

Larry had five chairs ready. The Aldens sat down

and started to peel potatoes.

Larry said, "We'll get through quicker this year with six workers. I always had three."

When the onions came around, Larry had big pails of water. "Peel the onions under water," he said. "If you don't, you will cry and not be able to see."

It was a fine idea, for there were many onions.

Next Larry and the Aldens got the clams out of their shells. They had piles and piles of clams.

"You should see this crowd eat," said Larry. "We have to have baked beans, too. Chowder isn't enough."

The beans were all baked ahead of time.

Henry said, "Too bad we can't get more food from the ocean." But if Larry heard him, he kept quiet.

At five o'clock the people began to come. It certainly looked as if everyone in town was there. Jessie had made paper caps for the family, to show that they were waiters. Other people helped, too.

Larry was a different boy. He smiled at everyone. He could hardly believe it when he saw Grandfather waiting on table in a paper hat.

One tall man was a summer visitor, just going through the town. He called Benny and said, "Sonny, ask the cook how he makes baked beans."

"He won't tell," said Benny. "A lot of people want to know. He always says, 'That is my secret.' The chowder is secret, too."

After the stranger had finished supper he went out to the kitchen tent to talk to Larry. But he did not learn how to bake the beans.

Larry was very polite and was willing to talk. But he said just what Benny had said—"That is my secret, sir."

"They say you like to cook," said the stranger.

"Oh, yes. Ever since I was fourteen I have cooked this supper. I love to cook. I like to put things together to see what will happen."

"Oh, do you? Do you go to college?"

"No." said Larry. He scowled.

The man saw the scowl, so he said goodbye to Larry and went down to his car. Nobody else noticed him very much. And nobody knew his name until some time later. Then they were really surprised.

CHAPTER 8

From the South Seas

I have an idea for today," said Mr. Alden at breakfast on Monday. "See this paper, Henry? In Ashland, the next town, ships come in from all over the world."

"From Blue Bay?" shouted Benny.

"Well, you are right," said Grandfather nodding at Benny. "They do come in from the South Seas. See, there is one coming in today. We might go over to Ashland and see her come in. She sailed from Tahiti and her name is Tahiti."

"Oh, boy!" cried Benny. "Maybe the captain will let us go over the ship."

"Maybe," agreed his grandfather. "It will be a beautiful passenger ship, not like the freighter you went to Blue Bay on."

"Very posh," said Benny.

"Yes, I guess that is the word," said Grandfather, smiling. "I know the company that owns that ship."

"Then I guess the captain will let us go on," said Jessie, looking at Violet. "Grandfather does know a lot of people."

"I don't know this captain, but I hear he is a very good man with a boat. He is young."

They washed the dishes and then got into the station wagon. Henry backed it out and they were soon on their way to Ashland.

"Boats are always late," said Jessie. "We may have to wait all day."

"Right," said Mr. Alden. "But there are seats on the wharf and a roof to keep the sun off. You will enjoy watching the small boats. They keep coming and going."

"How do you know so much about Ashland?" asked Henry. "I never heard of that town."

"Well, remember I grew up on Aunt Jane's farm. And I have been up here with Mr. Carter a few times. I am interested in that Tahiti boat."

"Ah, I thought so," said Jessie. "That's why we are going to see it come in."

Mr. Alden laughed. "I like to see ships come in anyway—any ship."

The Tahiti was late.

"I told you boats are always late," said Jessie.

They all sat down and watched the small boats. There was one big empty place for the Tahiti. Small boats came in to get gas and water.

"See that man having his breakfast on that boat?" said Jessie. "He has bacon and eggs."

"Now his wife is bringing the toast," said Violet. "It must be fun to cook and eat on a boat like that."

One boat had children climbing all over the deck. "Oh, they'll fall in!" cried Violet.

"I don't think so," replied Grandfather. "Those children are used to a boat."

The mother heard this. She looked up at Grandfather and laughed. She said, "Don't you worry.

All these children have been living on a boat since they were born. They can all swim and dive."

Everything was interesting, but still the ship did not come in. At last it was time for lunch.

"We had better get lunch at some place over here," said Mr. Alden. "We'll hear the boat whistle if it comes in."

It seemed good to eat at a real table again. The Aldens had a good lunch and finished with apple pie. Then they went back to the wharf.

"She's coming, sir," said a man in uniform. "She has passed the Point."

"Good!" said Mr. Alden. "Thanks for telling me."

Many men began to come down on the wharf to help tie up the big ship. Soon they saw it coming in the distance. It was pure white.

"It has three big whistles," said Violet.

"No, Vi, those are not whistles," said Benny. "They are smokestacks. See the smoke?"

Violet laughed at her mistake.

The big ship came nearer and nearer. It was very beautiful. A small boat went out to meet it. Then it slowly came into the empty place at the wharf. People were standing and waving at the rail of the ship. Then Jessie noticed that many people had come down to meet them. It was exciting to watch them. And Larry Cook was in the crowd. But it seemed as if he did not want to be seen. He never looked toward the Aldens.

"Is that the captain?" asked Benny.

"Yes. You can tell by his uniform."

After the crowd had gone, Grandfather went up to the captain and said, "Good day, sir. I am James Alden."

"Are you indeed?" said the captain. "I'm glad to meet you at last."

"These are my grandchildren. I wonder if they could go aboard," said Mr. Alden.

"Certainly," said the young man, smiling. "My name is Snow. I'll have an officer show them around."

"I don't want to take up your time," said Mr. Alden.

"Oh, no," said Captain Snow. "I have three days' leave. I live just over in Conley."

"Conley!" said Benny. "That's where we are staying. In the lighthouse."

"What an adventure that must be," said Captain Snow, "living in a lighthouse. Here is an officer. He will show you over the Tahiti."

The officer showed them everything. They looked in the boiler room, the swimming pool, the dining room, the cabins. Everything was much nicer than the Sea Star that had taken them to Blue Bay.

"Have you a big kitchen?" asked Violet.

"Kitchen? Oh, yes! We call it a galley. We feed hundreds of people. It takes a lot of pans and dishes, ranges, and an enormous refrigerator to do that. Come this way, and you will see."

The refrigerator was interesting because it was as big as a small room. There were two men in it,

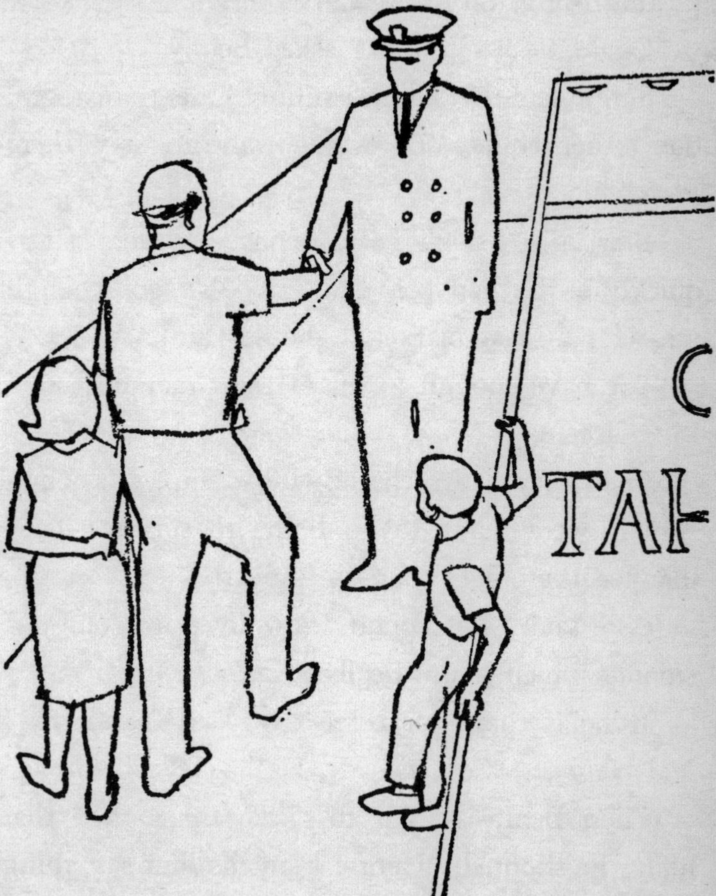

putting things on the many shelves.

"Could we go in, too?" asked Benny.

"Sure," said the officer, smiling. "Plenty of room, but rather cold. You won't want to stay there long."

"Brrr! No, I don't," said Benny. He went out as quickly as he had come in. "You've got enough meat for a meat market, I should think."

"We have enough for many meat markets," said the officer.

When they had seen the whole ship, the young Aldens were ready to go home to supper. They thanked the officer four times over.

Jessie said, "If Captain Snow lives in Conley, I wonder which house he lives in."

"If he is there for three days, we'll find out," said Henry. "We'll ask Mr. Hall. He will know."

When Benny started to climb up to bed that night, he shouted, "Henry, I am the dumbest thing in the world!"

"Why are you dumb?" Henry shouted back.

"Because I saw two or three long white bags in that refrigerator, just the kind you get plankton in, and I never said a word about it."

"Yes, old boy, I'm dumb, too, because I saw those bags and just didn't pay any attention. I was thinking about that refrigerator that we could walk into."

"I saw them, too," said Jessie. "Aren't we all dumb? We could have asked the officer what they had them for."

Grandfather said, "Now just what are you talking about?"

Benny called down the stairs, "Don't you remember, Grandfather, that's the way to get plankton? To drag a long bag through the South Seas?"

"Of course I remember. Captain Snow was getting plankton for Larry. I should say the whole family was quite stupid."

"Dumb," said Benny.

"All right. If you like it better—dumb," said Grandfather.

CHAPTER 9

Who Needs a Friend?

The Alden family did not stay dumb for long.

Tuesday Benny said, "Let's see if we can find out where Captain Snow lives."

"Just step down to the store," said Henry, laughing.

Everyone laughed.

"Wait just a minute until we finish the breakfast dishes," said Jessie, "and we can all go."

It was Grandfather who asked Mr. Hall, "Do you know Captain Snow of the Tahiti?"

"I'll say I know him," said Mr. Hall. "I've known him ever since he was a boy. He's brother to the Cook boy's mother."

"Aha!" said Jessie.

"Aha!" said Benny. "That explains a lot of things."

Mr. Hall leaned on the counter. "Larry always goes over to see his uncle when the Tahiti comes in. His uncle gives him something every time, but nobody has ever found out what it is."

"Maybe he gets it in a covered pail," said Benny, looking at Mr. Hall.

"How did you know that?" asked Mr. Hall.

"I saw him come home late one night and he had a pail," said Benny.

"Sometimes his uncle gives him a box," said Mr. Hall, "and sometimes a glass can. What do you suppose is in all those things?"

"We think we know," said Henry. "It's seaweed or plankton."

"And what's plankton, young feller?"

"It doesn't grow here close to shore," said Violet.

"It grows in the deep sea," said Henry. "In some places the deep sea is full of it."

"And what is it?" asked Mr. Hall.

"It's what a whale eats," said Benny. "It's plants and tiny fish and eggs and stuff you can't see without a microscope, but whales live on it. The whale takes a big mouthful and swallows the plankton and strains the water out of his mouth."

"Fishes eat it, too," Henry added. "It's something like the way land animals feed on growing plants and smaller animals."

"Plankton tastes awful," said Benny. "They say there's enough plankton in the deep sea to feed the world."

"You don't say!" said Mr. Hall. "Too bad it doesn't taste good. But what I want to know is what the Cook boy wants it for."

"We think he studies it and experiments with it," said Henry.

"He's a smart boy all right," said Mr. Hall. "Maybe Captain Snow would know."

"Where does he live?" asked Henry.

"Way up the street," said Mr. Hall. "Do you know where they're fixing the driveway?"

"Yes, that's where we got our cement," said Jessie.

Mr. Hall said, "There's a white house near that corner and that's Captain Snow's. He lives with his mother."

Benny said, "But most of the time he's out at sea."

"Yes," said Mr. Hall. "Most of the time."

Then Watch began to wag his tail. He went to the door.

A tall man came in and said, "Well, hello, dog. You are a good watchdog. Your name ought to be Watch."

"It is!" cried everybody.

"You're Captain Snow of the Tahiti," said Benny. "We were just coming down to see you."

"Good," said Captain Snow. "You are the Aldens who went over my ship. Just give me some crackers and five pounds of sugar, Mr. Hall. Then I'll go right home."

"Do you have to go home?" asked Benny.

"No, I'm not in a hurry. I'm on leave from ship just now."

"Can you come and sit on our rocks for a while?" asked Henry. "Right over there," he pointed.

"Certainly," said Captain Snow. "I'll leave the crackers and get them on the way home." All this time he had his hand on Watch's head.

"Watch likes you," said Violet.

"I like dogs," said Captain Snow.

"Let's go," said Benny. "We have five chairs and a table made of rocks."

"I'll sit on the table," said the captain.

"No, Henry will sit on the table," said Jessie. "His chair will fit you."

Soon they were sitting on the rocks, talking.

"You see that little house?" said Jessie, pointing to the little white house. "It was a summer kitchen for the lighthouse."

Henry added, "Mr. Cook, Larry's father, owns it now. That's what Mr. Hall told us."

"I see that it's empty," said the Captain.

"But it isn't empty," said Benny. "That's where

Larry does his experiments—at least we think so. He stays up most of the night. We don't know how he gets in—he can't have a key."

"I always wondered where he worked," said Captain Snow. "He doesn't tell me much, but I know he's trying to study by himself."

"He wants to go to college this fall," said Jessie.

"Everyone in town knows that," said the captain, laughing. "His father didn't catch on that Larry was so smart and let him write letters to two colleges."

"Did they want him?" asked Benny.

"Yes, they both wanted him," said the captain. "They wanted a young man who has tried to carry on experiments in science by himself."

Then Grandfather said, "I think he can get the work he wants at Henry's college. I might talk to the teachers there about him."

"Both colleges he wrote to wanted him. He chose Adams," said the captain.

"That's Henry's very college," shouted Benny.

"What do you know about that!" said Henry.

"If he went there, you could take care of him, Henry," said Benny.

Henry laughed. "He won't need anybody to take care of him," he said.

"But you could be his friend," said Violet.

"He'll need a friend," said Captain Snow. "So far his father has said *no*."

"But why?" said Benny. "And why does Larry have to hide his work?"

Captain Snow said, "I will tell you that. Tom Cook is a selfish man with a quick temper, but I think he really does love Larry."

"He doesn't show it much," said Benny.

"No, that's the trouble with them both," agreed the captain. "I think Larry is afraid his father would spoil his experiments if he knew about them."

"Larry cooked a wonderful supper," said Violet. "We heard his father was proud of him. He made five hundred dollars for the street lights."

Captain Snow got up. He said, "Well, I'll try to help him all I can. I know how interested he is in science. And he seems to have found some good friends."

After a minute Henry said, "Now the next thing is to make Larry really friendly."

"How?" asked Jessie.

Violet said, "He is a little friendly now, but that's because we helped him with the supper."

"What could we do, Grandfather?" asked Jessie. "Something that would give him a good time?"

"Wait till morning," said Mr. Alden. "Something may come up."

Something did come up. And it was very different from anything they had thought of.

CHAPTER 10

Hints and Plans

The next morning Jessie looked at Violet. "What in the world is the matter with you?" she asked.

"Mosquitoes," said Violet. Her face was red and puffed.

"Does your face hurt?" asked Jessie. "I would hardly know you. We'll have to do something."

"I can hardly open my mouth," said Violet.

"I heard the mosquitoes," said Jessie. "Look at my arm."

The boys came down to breakfast.

"Hello! Hello!" said Benny. "What happened to you, Violet? You look fat in the face."

"Mosquito bites," said Jessie.

"I had some, too," said Mr. Alden. "The wind has changed. Now it comes off the land. That always means mosquitoes."

Henry said slowly, "We have five windows."

"We have a screen door but no screens on the windows," said Benny. "I have an idea. Let's put screen cloth on the windows and get Larry to help us."

"And what about poor Violet?" asked Mr. Alden.

"Mr. Hall will have something for her bites," said Jessie. "I hope he has screen cloth, too."

Violet could hardly eat.

Henry said, "I've finished breakfast. I'll run over to the store."

Soon he came back with a great many things. He had something for Violet's face, a roll of screen cloth, a big box of tacks, and two small hammers.

Jessie covered Violet's face with white stuff from Mr. Hall's.

"You don't need to help, Violet," said Benny. "You can't see the tacks."

"The next thing is to find Larry," said Jessie. "Now, Benny, don't say anything about seeing him out in his father's boat. And don't ask him about what he does in the summer kitchen. He'll tell us when he's ready."

Benny said, "Oh, Jessie, I'm not *that* dumb."

The Aldens walked up and down the street and looked at Larry's house. Mrs. Cook was out in the yard.

"Where's Larry?" asked Henry.

"I don't know. He's out."

They could see that the Sea Cook was in.

At last they went down to the wharf. There was Larry, reading a book.

"Hi, Larry," shouted Benny. "Will you come and help us?"

"What doing?" asked Larry, shutting his book. "And where is the other sister?"

"You wouldn't know her," said Benny. "She is all mosquito bites. One eye is all shut."

Jessie said, "We want to put screens on five windows."

"You don't need me," said Larry.

"Count us," said Benny. "We have five windows and four people."

Larry laughed. He got up, put his book under his arm, and they all walked down the street.

Larry looked at the high windows. Then he looked at the screen cloth. "You can't put this on from the outside," he said.

"No," said Benny. "We are going to put it on from the inside. We'll show you. We have done it before."

"I'd like to see how you do it," said Larry.

Then Violet came out.

"I'm very sorry about your face," said Larry. Then he began to cut screen cloth.

Grandfather sat out on the rocks. He laughed to himself. Everyone was tapping or cutting. Grandfather could hear them talking. Once he heard Larry laugh. Then he got up quietly and went to the store.

Grandfather said to Mr. Hall, "Do you think Larry Cook would like steak?"

"Steak?" said Mr. Hall, "I don't think he ever had much."

"We'll try it then," said Grandfather. "Five pounds of steak should be enough."

"Potato chips," said Mr. Hall.

"Pickles," said Grandfather.

"How about a pie?" said Mr. Hall.

"I'll need rolls and two pies," said Grandfather. "Make them cherry."

Mr. Hall put all the food in a big bag. Grandfather went quietly back to the rocks. He could hear that the pounding had stopped. He found two pieces of old iron. He hit them together. It sounded like a bell. Grandfather looked up and saw Benny at his window.

"Is that a dinner bell, Grandfather?" shouted Benny.

"Come down and see," said Grandfather.

Laughing, they all ran to the rocks. Grandfather showed them what he had bought.

"We'll need a fire for that steak," said Larry.

"Right," said Henry. "Here's our fireplace. We can use our grill."

Everyone began to gather dry wood, but it was Larry who built the fire.

The Aldens noticed that Larry never looked toward the summer kitchen. He did not know that they already knew a great deal about something that interested him very much.

"I forgot you were a cook," said Benny.

"How do you like your steak?" asked Larry. "Well done?"

"No, he likes it burned up," said Henry.

"He won't get any burned up steak from me," said Larry.

"I want mine very rare, my boy," said Mr. Alden.

"I know," said Larry. "Rare but not raw."

"Good!" said Mr. Alden. "I shall enjoy this meal."

They could hardly wait for the fire to burn down, but Larry would not put the steaks on. At last the fire was just right. Larry counted, "Two rare, three medium, and Benny's well done."

"That means I'll have to wait till last," said Benny.

Jessie put butter on the rolls. Mr. Alden's steak was done first. Larry took his own off and moved the rest to the hot part of the fire. Soon everyone was eating a steak sandwich.

"Poor Grandfather," said Benny. "No coffee."

"I don't need coffee today," said Grandfather. "Just give me a pickle."

When they had picked up after lunch, Larry began to think he should go home. He said, "I had a fine time." He looked at Violet and smiled. "I hope you'll have no mosquitoes."

"Thank you for helping us," said Violet. "Come again soon."

"Maybe I will," said Larry.

After he had gone, Jessie said, "I think we are really friends with Larry now. Don't you, Grandfather?"

"Yes," said Mr. Alden. "You did exactly right.

You gave him something interesting to do. Then you all worked together. That's the best way to make friends."

"Well," said Benny, "I wish that we'd get to be such good friends that Larry would tell us about his work. Maybe he thinks he can sell that stuff and get rich."

"I think he's more interested in it as science work," said Henry. "But that's just a guess."

Then they all sat looking at the beautiful blue sea. Violet said, "It never seems to rain here. Every single day has been sunny. I wonder why?"

"Yes," said Mr. Alden. "So far it has been sunny for three weeks. But you will find it isn't always that way. In fact I think I feel a storm coming up now."

"I don't," said Benny. "There isn't a cloud in the sky."

"Maybe not today," said Grandfather, "but soon. It is lucky we have a nice tight lighthouse to stay in. We'll see some big waves."

"Oh, I love big waves," said Violet. "They are so beautiful dashing on the rocks. And we are right by the water—almost in the water."

The storm did not come that night. The family had supper on the rocks. They had a fine night with no mosquitoes.

"Pretty good screens," said Benny.

All the next day they swam or sat on the beach in the sun. Then the family had supper on the rocks. Just as they finished, Grandfather said, "Look! The storm! The wind has changed!"

Sure enough, clouds were speeding across the sky.

Jessie and Henry gathered the supper things together.

They hurried into the lighthouse just as the first drops began to fall.

"Just a little rain," said Benny, laughing. "It feels good on my head. I like to get my hair wet."

CHAPTER 11

A Wild Storm

When the Aldens had shut all the windows and looked out at the sea, they changed their minds about the rain. This was no little rain. This was a storm.

The sky became very dark. There was thunder. The rain fell in sheets. The wind made a terrible noise around the lighthouse.

"You do know about the weather, Grandfather," said Benny. "You said a storm was coming, and boy! here is a storm."

"There goes a telephone pole," shouted Henry. "Nobody can telephone out of this town tonight."

"I hope no one is out in a boat," said Violet. "The waves would tip it over."

The waves dashed up against the lighthouse. They even ran down the road and covered it with water.

The storm grew worse. Lightning made the whole beach light. The thunder sounded very loud over the water.

"I don't care for this at all," said Violet. "It seems dangerous."

"It is dangerous," said Grandfather quietly. "I surely hope nobody is out in a boat."

The storm did not stop. It grew even worse. The waves covered the whole wide beach. Suddenly there was a loud knock at the door.

"Who in the world is *that*?" shouted Benny. "I hate to open the door. The rain will pour in."

But Henry opened the door. It was Mr. Cook.

"Have you seen my son?" he cried. "Where is my son?"

"Come in, quick!" said Henry. "We don't know where your son is. We haven't seen him today."

"Oh, oh!" cried the man. "My wife told me to look in the little house first, but he isn't there. He must have taken my boat! He's out in my boat! What shall I do? He will tip over. Nobody could handle a boat in this storm!"

Henry said, "Is there any Coast Guard around here?"

"In Ashland," Tom Cook cried. "They haven't time to get here."

"We'll see about that," said Henry. He dragged on his raincoat and went to open the door.

"Where are you going, Henry?" asked Grandfather sharply.

"I'm going for the Coast Guard. The telephone's out. We can't do a thing alone."

Mr. Alden opened his mouth. Then he shut it again. He knew Henry had to go.

Henry was backing the car around. "Get in," said Henry to Mr. Cook. "Quick!" And off he drove through the water that covered the road, splashing it high as he went.

After Henry and Mr. Cook had gone, Mr. Alden was very quiet.

At last Violet said, "Henry will make it. He always does."

"I hope you're right, child," said Mr. Alden. "I am worried. If Larry is out in the open sea in this, I don't see how he can ever get to land."

"Maybe he knows the weather, too," said Jessie. "Maybe he started out for home before the storm came."

"How awful that the light in this lighthouse is gone!" said Benny. "If we could only light that, he could find his way better."

"The reflector is left," said Jessie. "Maybe a small light would show a little."

Everyone had a flashlight that would stand up. Benny carried them all to his room at the top and set them around. The reflector did show a little light through the storm.

By this time they heard voices outside. The neighbors had come to the lighthouse to find out about the Cook boy. They all knew his father's boat was gone.

"Come in, everybody," said Jessie. Everyone was dripping with water. "My brother has gone for the

Coast Guard. They will go out from Ashland and look for Larry."

Then Jessie and Violet saw Mrs. Cook. She looked pale, but she smiled at the girls.

The neighbors were wonderful. They had seen storms before. A woman told Jessie to heat a lot of water and make coffee for the Coast Guard men. She herself helped.

The men who had come went out on the beach to see if they could see anything. They stood in the waves up to their knees. But soon the water was up to their waists. They went back to the rock seats. They all had flashlights and some had enormous field glasses.

"The Coast Guard is quick," said Mrs. Cook. "They will be out to sea before your brother can get home."

Jessie and Violet put their arms around her.

The light in the top of the lighthouse showed a little through the heavy rain. It seemed like ten years before a man shouted, "I see the Coast Guard boat! And I see the Cook boat!"

Henry and Tom Cook drove up as the man spoke.

"Oh, where?" begged Mr. Cook, getting out. "Show it to me."

The man gave him his glasses and told him which way to look. The boats were still right side up, but they often disappeared in the waves. Then Henry went down to the beach, too.

"What will they do?" Henry asked.

"They'll take the boy off and tie his boat to the Coast Guard boat. I hope they will see our light and come here to our beach. The little boat can get through the waves here."

Men looked through their glasses. "They're tying the boat on now. They must have the boy."

"If I ever get my son back, he can have anything he wants," cried Tom Cook. "Anything at all. Anything in the world!"

"He's a smart boy, your Larry," said Henry. "Maybe you know that."

"Yes, I know that. If he only comes back safe!"

"He will," said a fisherman. "The Coast Guard is coming fast this way. They wouldn't come now if they didn't have the boy aboard."

"Oh, thank you!" cried Mr. Cook. "Can you really see their boat?"

"See for yourself." The fisherman gave him his glasses. The rain was still pouring down. It was still thundering. Everyone was soaking wet. But they could see the Coast Guard coming through the great waves. The Sea Cook II was tied on behind it.

Mrs. Cook helped Jessie heat towels and blankets in front of the gas oven and make a bed with the blankets.

"You'll have to use my bed for him," said Mr. Alden.

Henry said, "You may have my bed, Grandfather, and I'll go up with Benny."

"I don't think I'm going to bed," said Mr. Alden.

"We'll be all ready for him when he comes," said Jessie.

"Is there a doctor in this town?" asked Mr. Alden.

"Oh, yes indeed. Someone has gone for him. He is on his way."

"Well, since there is no policeman," said Mr. Alden, "I thought there wouldn't be any doctor either."

"He is a very good doctor. His name is Dr. Phillips."

"That big Coast Guard boat can't land here," said Henry to a man.

"No, they will come to the beach in the smaller boat. The Coast Guard can run it through the waves. You'll see."

Nearer and nearer came the big boat. The storm was still raging. When the boat was quite near it stopped. Three of the men got into the Sea Cook II and rowed for the beach. Larry was lying in the boat.

At last the boat reached the shore. Strong men took hold of it, and pulled it up on the sand.

Henry helped. He looked at Larry. He was lying still with his eyes shut.

"He's alive," the man said. "But he doesn't know anything yet. Put him to bed and get a doctor. We saw your dim light."

"We're all ready," said Henry. "Right in the lighthouse."

"The lighthouse!" said the man.

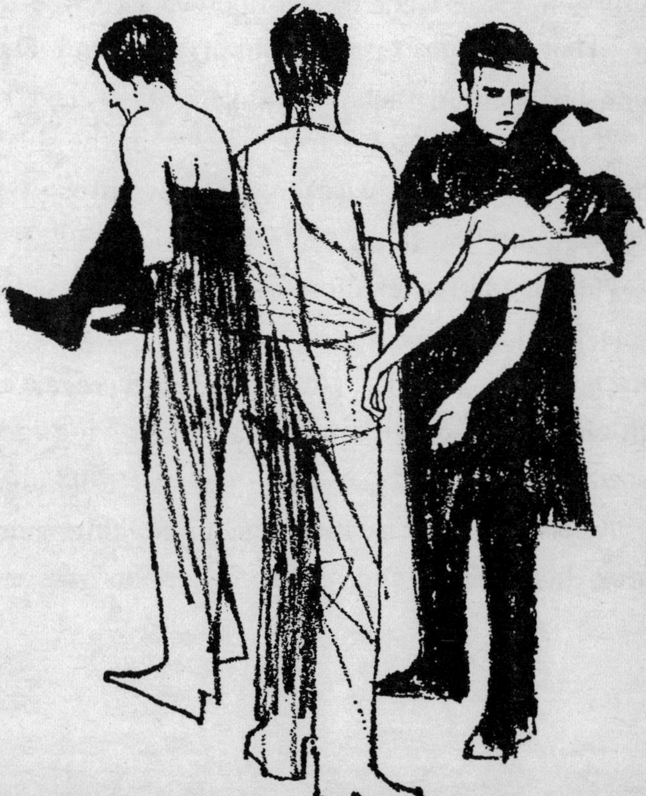

"Yes, we are living there this summer. We have a bed all made up for him with hot blankets."

Henry helped the men lift Larry out of the boat. He was soaked and his hair was dripping wet. The men took him into the lighthouse.

"We'll get him dry first," they said. Mrs. Cook rubbed Larry's hair with a hot towel. He was shivering, but he did not open his eyes.

When Jessie went to the door to meet the doctor, the men got Larry's dripping clothes off and wrapped him in the hot blankets. They laid him in Grandfather's bed.

Everyone came in with the doctor to see how Larry was. Suddenly Larry shouted, "Feed the world! Feed the whole world!"

Henry looked at Jessie.

The doctor said, "He has a high fever. He doesn't know what he is saying."

Violet did not say a word. She was thinking.

Tom Cook was at Larry's side, begging him to open his eyes.

"Larry, Larry," he kept saying.

The doctor said, "I don't think you ought to talk to him. He will wake up himself when he is able. Remember he has been out in that terrible storm. It is better for him to keep quiet now."

Mr. Cook did not say another word. But he never moved from Larry's side.

Jessie began to think. "Isn't it funny?" she thought. "We were sure Mr. Cook didn't like his own son. And we find he does. Maybe we'll find out that Larry likes his father, too."

When Larry could swallow, the doctor gave him some medicine. A little color came back in his face.

"Have you any hot soup?" the doctor asked Jessie. "Soon he will be able to take it. It will do him good."

"Yes, I have canned soup," said Jessie.

"That's all right. Don't put much water in it. Give it to him strong."

Larry's mother was the one to feed him the soup. His eyes opened and then shut. Then he opened them again. He seemed to be hungry.

All this time, Benny had not said a single word. He just watched. Now he sat down quietly in a chair. Watch went over and sat close beside him.

The old dog did not bark once at all the strangers. He seemed to know that they were Jessie's friends. So they would be his friends, too. Benny put his arm around the dog's neck and together they sat there.

Violet went and put her arm around Benny's shoulders. "It's been too exciting, Benny," she said. "You'll feel better soon. Suppose you have some hot soup, too."

Benny was thankful to eat the hot soup. He almost went to sleep eating it.

"Better lie down," said Violet. "After all, it's almost midnight."

Benny was soon fast asleep.

All the rest stayed up and watched Larry. All at once he said, "Mother, I tried to feed the whole world."

"What is he talking about?' asked Dr. Phillips. "Keep him quiet if you can. He will soon be asleep. Don't try to take him home yet."

The kind neighbors began to say goodnight.

"I'll come again early in the morning," said Dr. Phillips, going out last of all.

Jessie and Violet went up to their room. Henry carried Benny upstairs to his bed without waking him. Mr. Alden and Watch sat quietly with Larry's father and mother. And for the first time, when the clock struck twelve at midnight, Watch did not bark.

CHAPTER 12

The Secret Is Out

The next day was beautiful. The storm had gone. Everyone got up early and went downstairs to see how Larry was. Dr. Phillips came early, too. Mr. and Mrs. Cook were still there, sitting by the bed.

"How is the boy?" asked Mr. Alden.

"He is very much better," said Dr. Phillips. "But he still doesn't know what he is talking about."

"Oh." said Benny, "I think he does."

"And I do, too," said Henry. "What is he saying?"

"Oh, the same old thing, about feeding the world. Will you tell me how that makes sense?"

"We'll *show* you," said Henry, "if it's all right with Larry. That is better than telling. Mr. Cook and Grandfather, you can come with the doctor, too."

"I don't need to come," said Mrs. Cook smiling, "I know all about it. I used to take Larry his supper every night. Here is a key. Your dog always barked and I was sure you'd come out and question me. I'll stay with Larry now."

"Eat anything you see," said Larry, almost smiling.

Then the Aldens led the men down the path to the little white house. Mr. Cook said, "I never guessed a thing."

Benny said, "Larry comes to work here every night. We thought we smelled fish cooking." They all went in.

"What is this?" said Dr. Phillips, picking up a little cake.

"Well," said Henry. "I rather think it is a cake made of seaweed. It was baked in that pan."

"Try it," said Benny. "Larry said we could." The doctor broke off a piece of the cake and tried it.

"How is it?" asked Benny.

"Not too bad, not too good," said the doctor.

"But why is Larry using seaweed?" asked Mr. Cook.

"There's a great deal of it," said Henry. "Anyone can get it free. It could be made into food people could eat. It would help feed the world."

The doctor said slowly, "I know the Japanese use it, but they like it. They make cakes and candy and puddings."

"That is exactly right," said Henry. "If we liked it, we could have all we wanted just for sending boats out after it."

Mr. Cook looked at Henry and said, "So that is what my boy was doing—trying to make seaweed taste good. He did know what he was talking about all the time."

"Then Larry is well if he is talking sense," said Dr. Phillips. "Only he is still weak. He can get up when he feels able."

Dr. Phillips went on his way, and the rest went back to Larry. He was sitting up eating his breakfast.

"Tell us, Larry, what you were trying to do," said Grandfather, sitting down beside the bed.

"Oh, it is so interesting!" cried Larry. "I had to do my experiments with seaweed because plankton wouldn't keep. Uncle Rich Snow always brought me some plankton from the South Seas. He had a refrigerator."

"We've been in that refrigerator," said Benny, laughing. "We saw your white bags of plankton, but we didn't know then what it was."

"I like to look at the plankton under my microscope. But I do wish I had a large microscope. The plankton would be so beautiful. It's all colors and so many different kinds, and so small you can't see it at all without the microscope."

"We saw some plankton when we went to Blue Bay," said Henry.

"Then you know. If we could only make it good to eat, it would feed the world."

"Tell us about your experiments," said Mr. Alden.

"Well, I have tried a good many things. Of course I don't have much to work with. I mixed the jelly of the seaweed with flour and sugar and made cakes and fried them. They were not very good. Next time I was going to put in flavoring."

"Good work!" said Mr. Alden. "You have done well all alone. Now you need help."

Then Grandfather went on talking to Mr. Cook. "If you will let Larry go to Adams College, I will help you pay for it."

"Oh, no," said Mr. Cook. "That isn't it! I have enough money. Captain Snow would have given us money, too. I just made up my mind that he couldn't go, and I hated to give in. You see I never had a chance for much schooling. I've done all right. I couldn't see why Larry needed to go to college. A waste of money, I thought." Mr. Cook stopped and then he added, "I guess I'm quick to lose my temper and slow to change my mind."

"I was like that, too," said Benny. "I used to howl my head off."

Mr. Cook laughed. He said, "And you think I am howling now? All right. He can go."

Jessie looked at Larry. His eyes were shining. He had forgotten his breakfast.

Mr. Alden said, "Let's all sit down and talk about this. This is wonderful of you, Mr. Cook. You see, I know Adams College. Henry goes there. They have a teacher who could help Larry on this very work. He will work with Larry, I am sure."

Larry sat up straight. Watch went over and put his paws on the bed and wagged his tail.

"That settles it," shouted Benny. "Now Larry is one of the family!"

CHAPTER 13

A Final Surprise

Grandfather sat forward in his chair.

"Another thing," he said. "We ought to go home soon."

"Oh, why?" asked Benny.

Mr. Alden laughed. "I have to work, for one thing."

Jessie said, "Oh, I suppose you do."

Henry said, "I must get ready for college, too."

"I shall miss you all," said Larry.

"You won't miss Henry," said Benny. "You'll see him every day at college."

"I can go back to my house this morning," said Larry. "I feel all right—only weak."

"I'll take you in the station wagon," said Henry, "and Mr. and Mrs. Cook, too."

Suddenly Mrs. Cook said, "Wait! I have an idea. You must all come to our house for supper."

Mr. Alden shook his head. "Better not, Mrs. Cook," he said. "You'll have enough to do taking care of Larry without cooking a supper for eight. But we'd enjoy it all right."

"I won't need a thing," said Larry. "I'll just lie down once in a while."

Mrs. Cook smiled. She said, "Larry isn't the only one in the family who can cook. I do it, too. And I like it."

The four young Aldens were looking at Grandfather, hoping he would change his mind.

"Very well," he said. "We'd love to come if you really feel that way."

"Good!" said Mrs. Cook. "Come about five and see our yard. We'll eat at six."

Benny said, "I won't eat much lunch, Mrs. Cook, so I can eat a lot of supper. I bet you are just as good a cooker as Larry."

They all laughed at Benny. "Really," he said, "I mean it. I'll eat hardly any lunch at all."

"I can't imagine it," said Henry.

"I'll get dressed," said Larry, "and go along home."

"You'll have to wear some of my clothes," said Henry. "Yours aren't dry yet."

After the Cook family had gone, Benny said, "Now I wonder what Mrs. Cook will have for supper. It won't be frankfurters, I'm sure."

"It won't be chowder," said Henry, smiling.

"It won't be hamburgers," Benny went on.

"Now, Benny," said Violet, "don't be talking about things to eat all the morning. You make me hungry already."

"What shall I do, then?"

"You might put up the clothes line. Tie it between the houses. We can get Larry's things dry in the sun."

"Shoes and all?" asked Benny.

"Yes. Tie the strings together and hang them over the line."

When the job was done, Benny came in again. "What shall I do now?" he asked.

"Oh, Benny," cried Jessie. "Go down to the beach and sit and watch the water. We're very busy."

Benny went slowly down to the beach. In a minute he shouted, "Oh, come quick! Millions of shells! Heaps and piles of shells! Bushels of shells!"

Everyone ran. They swept the shells and shoveled the shells into anything that would hold them. They set them on the rock table. As Mr. Alden worked he said, "I think we're going to make it. These shells were washed up by the storm. They came from far away."

The water came in steadily. At last almost every shell was saved.

"We won!" cried Benny. "Now the tide can come in."

"And now we'll have fun," said Mr. Alden. "See if you can find an empty pan."

"Here's a kettle," said Violet.

"Just the thing, child," said Mr. Alden. "I think it will be full."

"What are you going to do?" asked Henry.

"I am going to pick over the shells and save the interesting ones," said his grandfather.

The children sat down to watch. At once Mr. Alden cried, "Here's a beautiful red scallop shell, and this black and white one came from far away.

These shells never grow around here. That is why some of them are broken."

Quickly Mr. Alden picked over the shells. He never stopped once.

"My!" said Benny. "You know a lot about shells."

"I ought to," said Mr. Alden. "I have studied them all my life. Isn't this shell beautiful?"

"Say!" cried Benny. "Doesn't it look something like an olive? And speaking of olives, I wonder if Mrs. Cook will have pickles? If she has hamburger she will have to have pickles."

"Now, Benny," said Henry, "stop talking about food. You know you are not hungry yet."

But all day long Benny was waiting for five o'clock to come. At quarter of five he said, "Don't you think we could go now? It will take us fifteen minutes to walk to Mrs. Cook's."

Henry said, "Oh, so we are going to walk, are we?"

"Henry and I will ride," said Mr. Alden.

"Wait five minutes more, Benny," said Henry, "and you can help me wipe off the car. Then we will go."

They reached the Cooks' house at exactly five o'clock. Mrs. Cook came around the house from the backyard. "You are just in time," she said. "Mr. Cook wants to show you our yard."

The Aldens were very much surprised when they saw the yard. It was beautiful. There were big bushes of flowers and beds filled with flowers. The grass was very green. In the middle was an enormous fireplace and a long table.

"She does have pickles," whispered Benny to Jessie. There were chairs around the table.

"We might as well eat," said Mrs. Cook. "We are all here."

"That's good," said Benny. "I've been hungy all day."

"We'll fill you up," said Mr. Cook.

Larry sat in a long chair. He looked weak, but he said he felt fine.

"You can help me, Henry," said Mrs. Cook. Henry came back from the house with a pan of rolls. They were light and brown. They smelled delicious.

Benny whispered again to Jessie, "I still wonder what we will have to go with the rolls."

He did not have to wait long. Mrs. Cook gave Henry two holders, and he lifted an enormous pan off the fire. The fire was almost out.

"Oh! Oh! Chicken legs!" yelled Benny. "I can eat a lot of those."

"How many can you eat?" asked Mrs. Cook.

"Well, four anyway," said Benny. "My friend Mike can eat eight."

"You can have eight, too, if you want," said Mrs. Cook, laughing.

But when Benny saw the watermelon, he ate only four chicken legs. Mr. Alden said, "Mrs. Cook, these are delicious. You can certainly cook as well as Larry."

Suddenly Larry looked toward the street. A big

car drove up quietly and stopped.

"We have more company, Mother," Larry said, pointing to the car.

"No," shouted Benny, "it's our company! It's Mr. Carter. He's getting out now."

And it was John Carter, one of the men who worked for Grandfather. He had a large black box. He carried it over to where everyone waited.

With a smile he said, "I felt lonesome, and after I read your letters I wanted to see Larry."

"Well, this is Larry," said Benny. "He is lying down in that long chair because he was almost drowned in the storm we had."

"I know," nodded Mr. Carter. "Your grandfather telephoned me." He shook hands and said hello to everybody.

All this time Larry looked at the box. He knew what was in it, but he could not believe it might be for him.

Mr. Carter was saying, "Here you are, Larry. From what Mr. Alden told me, I guess you need a bigger microscope. Mine has just been lying around. I haven't used it for years now that I'm not with the F.B.I. You may keep it."

Benny carried the box over to Larry for him to open.

Larry's hands shook so that Benny said, "Maybe your hands are shaking because you almost drowned."

"No," said Larry, and his voice shook, too. "It's because I'm so glad to have a good microscope. I can never thank you enough, Mr. Carter, never!"

"Don't try," said Mr. Carter. He and the Aldens were glad to see how pleased Larry was.

"Well, Carter," said Grandfather, "you didn't come way up here just to give Larry that microscope. You must have had some other reason."

Mr. Carter laughed and said, "Well, so I did. I thought I might help you pack. And I brought you a letter from Adams College. It is from a Dr. William Steere."

Grandfather read the letter at once. "Good," he

said. "Excellent. Larry, this Dr. Steere wants a boy like you very much."

"Why, sir?" asked Larry.

"Because he is doing the same work that you are. He is experimenting with seaweed and plankton for food."

"Wonderful!" said Larry. "I'd like to work with him."

"He says something else," said Grandfather. "He says that we ought to spend more money getting food from the sea instead of bothering with space."

"I think so, too," said Larry. "I suppose we ought to do both. But I am more interested in the sea. Think how deep it is. Miles and miles. And all full of food if we can only get it."

Mr. Cook put his hand on his son's shoulder. He said, "I can see that you and Dr. Steere will get along fine."

John Carter had already eaten, but he had a large piece of watermelon just the same.

When the time came to say good-by to the

Cooks, Henry said, "We go back to our real home tomorrow. We're sorry to go."

"And we are sorry to see you leave," Mrs. Cook said.

"But I'll see you soon," Larry called, "at college."

The next day Mr. Carter was a great help. He worked with the girls on the packing and he took some of the bags in his own car.

Benny ran to Mr. Hall's store to give him the lighthouse keys. When he came back, the family was ready to go.

"I want to ride with Mr. Carter," said Benny.

"Very well," said Grandfather. "No reason not to, if Mr. Carter wants you."

Mr. Carter laughed and said he wanted company. The girls and Grandfather rode with Henry.

They drove past Mr. Hall's to wave good-by and then past the Cooks before leaving Conley.

At last home again, they told Mrs. McGregor, the housekeeper, all about their adventures.

Mr. Carter told how well the young people had

solved the mystery. "I couldn't have done better," he said.

"Oh, yes, you could," said Jessie. "You used to be an F.B.I. man."

"No, really, I couldn't," said Mr. Carter. "Larry would trust young people more than he would a man. I'm sure of that. You were wonderful with Larry."

"That's right, John," said Grandfather, nodding. "They were."

The bags were unpacked and Henry took the empty car around to the garage.

But the family did not sit around very long doing nothing. Everyone was busy in what was left of the summer.

One day Grandfather and Henry went to a store to get Henry clothes for fall. But Grandfather bought two jackets, not just one. Henry tried them on and said they were just right. One was gray and one was brown. The brown one went into a special box to be mailed to Larry Cook.

Henry wrote a letter saying it was the kind of jacket all the boys wore at Adams.

Then the time came when Henry and Larry went to Adams College. Grandfather went, too. He took the boys into the dean's office and told him who Larry was.

Larry sat down near the door. It was half open.

Suddenly Larry stood up looking very much surprised. A tall man came in. He looked at Larry once. Then he looked again. Then he held out his hand and said, "Well, well! Clam chowder!"

Larry cried, "Baked beans!" The two shook hands.

"What in the world are you two talking about?" asked Mr. Alden. "Do you know Larry?"

"Yes," said the tall stranger. "I know he makes the best clam chowder and baked beans that I ever ate!"

The dean laughed. He said, "That makes my work easier, if you know each other. Larry, this is Dr. Steere."

"Dr. Steere!" cried Larry. "The one I am going

to work for?"

"The very one," said the dean. "Sit down, Dr. Steere. This is Mr. Alden, and this is Henry Alden. They brought Larry along to meet you."

Dr. Steere looked at Larry. He said, "I have seen your papers that you did all alone. You are already doing college work. I will be glad to help you because our work may be important to the whole world."

"I hope so," said Larry. "It seems important to me."

Mr. Alden looked at his watch. "I must go," he said. "You two boys find your rooms and Henry's friends, and good luck to you both."

Mr. Alden shook hands with Larry. He said, "You have a wonderful teacher, my boy. I know you will do well."

Mr. Alden left and then Dr. Steere left. The boys went to find their rooms and the dean sat alone.

"I like a boy like that Larry," he thought. "And he has a fine friend in Henry Alden."

About a month later, Grandfather got a wonderful letter from Henry.

"Read it out loud," said Jessie.

This is what Mr. Alden read:

Dear Grandfather and All,

Larry and I are so excited! Dr. Steere likes Larry's work. He has asked him to stay here at the college all summer and work with him. But Larry thinks he shouldn't do that. He wants to be with his father in the summer. So what do you think? Dr. Steere says he will come to the little white house in Conley and work with Larry. They will fix up the little house and put on a new room. Dr. Steere says he will call it "Cook's Experiments." Isn't that wonderful? He thinks some day Larry will be famous.

I have to tell you that Larry wears his white lab coat all the time. He almost never wears his jacket.

The boys like him and think he is smart.

Love to everybody,

HENRY

"What wonderful news," said Jessie. "Aren't we glad we made friends with Larry Cook?"

"I am very much pleased with you," said Grandfather. "You young people changed a cross young bear into a fine young man."

"I think Benny did that mostly," said Jessie.

"Well, I don't," said Benny. "I think we all did it together—and you, Grandfather, and Captain Snow and Watch."

"Don't forget Mr. Hall," said Jessie.

"We'll never forget Mr. Hall," said Violet.

"No, sir!" said Benny. "Mr. Hall knows absolutely everything!"